Elegy

For

Flowers:

Poetry From a Wilted Garden

Copyright 2025 by S.E. Sumpter

First Edition May 2025

Print ISBN: 9798285105640

Book Cover by S.E. Sumpter

Photography by S.E. Sumpter

For Ted, and your endless love for me. You are the personification of the time I needed to heal the broken parts of me I never thought I could fix.

-Tails

Notes From The Author

We're all just torn open and
bleeding out words,
hoping someone buries their
hands in our wounds
so they too understand why our
pens are stained red.

Death

I cannot recall a time before me. All the things I have touched have withered away and returned to the Earth beneath my feet.

Grief

I remain felt but never seen. All the lives I've touched have drowned in tears.

Time

I am not an illusion; I am only
what I am—the holder of days
that have come and gone.

This is something else entirely...

Love may live here,
but so does Death.

Love may remain,
but so does Grief.

Love may surpass all,
but so does Time.

Table of Contents

This

is

not

a

garden.

It

is

a

graveyard.

Death

I'm just trying to survive, as Death holds my head above water. She keeps telling me it's not time, but God, it feels like it's past due.

The scariest things in life,

are the demons we cannot see

the help we cannot hear coming

and the fear we feel

when we are alone in the dark.

Middle Child Syndrome

I feel like I'm on the edge of a cliff
and I can't find it in me not to jump,
my lungs want to engulf the salty water
and replace the oxygen keeping me alive.

No one told me that in this life
I would be begging for it to end,
I'm afraid I've reached the bottom
and there's nowhere left to go.

I'm screaming for relief
and it feels like there's none left for me
like I'm God's middle child
somehow always forgotten.

The gates don't seem as golden
when you've been to the edge of His creation
and struck a match
to burn it all down with grief.

Not all the angels in Heaven
or even the demons in Hell
could help me find my way,
but I'll make sure they know my name.

How long did anyone expect me to bend
before I broke into a million shards,
because no one was there
to tell me it would be alright
that I could step away,
that there would be somewhere safe
where I could not be okay.

Highway

It was nighttime
and I was standing on the edge of the road
thinking about stepping into the lights.
I picked up my foot
to move closer to the asphalt
as cars rushed past me,
everything was a blur.

All I could hear was my heart
pounding in my ears
and the sound of my rapid breathing.
I wasn't even aware I was hyperventilating.

Could I do it?
I felt like I was past my breaking point,
but still,
has it come to this?

I don't think anyone would have thought-
thought I would be that person,
the person who couldn't control themself
and walked into oncoming traffic.

But I wanted to be that person
in that single moment
I closed my eyes,
and I wanted to kiss Death.

But Death told me,
not today,
and I turned
and walked away.

Still thinking,
what if I made a mistake?

I Just Survived The Day

Yesterday was hard.
I imagined what it would feel like to be hit by a car
but I walked away from the road.
I imagined what it would be like
if I wasn't here anymore
but I took my allotted pills
and turned out the lights.
I imagined what would happen
if I didn't wake up in the morning
but went to bed and prayed that I did.

Today was hard.
I felt like running away again
but I tucked my bags under the bed.
I felt like hurting myself again
but I put the knife back down.
I felt like being anywhere else but here again
but I stayed.

Tomorrow will be hard.
I'll have to get up and fight to be here
because every day is the same,
haunted by the thought of what would happen
if
I didn't survive the day.

Trapped

I'm stuck in a bad place,
I want to cry
to call out in pain,
but I am silently shaking
and that is somehow,
so much worse.

Drowning doesn't begin to cover
the feeling of suffocation
that's hindering my lungs.
I'm spirling inside,
I know it,
but on the outside
I'm standing completely still.

My heart is breaking
and if I tear a hole in my chest,
tiny pieces of me would come tumbling out
and crash upon the floor,
staining it red.

I feel trapped in a place I don't belong,
condemned behind the same glass
that had kept me hostage my whole life.
Yet even after all this time,
here I am,
still screaming at the top of my lungs
and no one can hear a sound.

I'm still bloodying my knuckles against this wall
as I have been for decades,
captive hands full of broken bones
but I still haven't even scratched the surface.

I'm beginning to lose my will to fight
to try to run away from the things that hurt me,
maybe I'd be better off
if they just consumed me instead.

Is there truly anything left to fight for
if I'm standing in a prison,
gasping for air,
when I can see the whole world on the other
side
but I'm still trapped here,
rattling chains
and gnawing at my own hands to be free.

Shattered Glass

That was the way I ended
with my heart splintered
into a million shards of glass,
crashing onto the floor.

I hated the way it sounded,
it was too gentle
too graceful
to be my demise.

The little pieces pinged on the tile
like tiny cries for help,
and that didn't sound like me at all.

As the blood in my veins ran dry,
I became a skeleton of who I once was
and eventually,
I dried up
crumbled
and blew away like dust in the wind.

Just like that,
it was the end of me.

Or so I thought.

The Sun

Some days,
I can feel the warmth of the sun
penetrate my soul,
and I let myself
just for a moment,
rest in the sunlight.

But I am not the foolish girl I once was.

You see,
the sun is not always so kind.
Too much warmth can kill you
and you don't even realize it,
until it's too late.

You get so comfortable
resting in the sun's rays of light,
that you forget,
those same rays are burning your skin
and peeling it from the bone.

No matter how beautiful it is
setting on the horizon,
remember the colors are brief,
the sun will leave you
draped in the cold darkness of the night,
and it'll feel like death.

Fleeing Hell

I was running for my life
hard and fast,
my faith had slipped through my fingers
and here,
miracles were nowhere to be found.
So I was on my own,
running,
trying to get back home.

There was no more oxygen in my lungs,
my legs begged for a break
but I kept running,
from a past that haunted me
and the demons inside my head,
that urged me to die.

But I wasn't ready to die yet.

So I ran faster,
I forced my heart to keep beating
my lungs to keep breathing
and my legs to keep going.

No matter the cost,
I wasn't going to stop
I wasn't going to die here.

I escaped from the devil himself
and now I was on the run
a wanted prisoner,
but without his shackles,
he knew he couldn't catch me.

I wasn't going to slip,
not again.

So I kept running
and I'll keep running
until I reach the light I'm after,
until Hell is just a bad memory
and Lucifer is nothing to me,
but the monster in my childhood closet.

<u>Whiskey</u>

Death shook me by the shoulders
and I rolled my eyes,
but I put the bottle down,
it was damn near empty anyways.
She shook her head at me
like she was telling me "no"
for the third time this week,
and it was only Wednesday.

I told her I didn't want to hear it,
especially not tonight.
"Just do it!" I pleaded with Death
standing in my kitchen,
frustrated,
drunk off whiskey
and I was at the mercy of Death herself,
to just do her job.

They say you add a few drops of water
and the whiskey tastes smoother.
I always added a few drops of tears instead,
made it taste like heartbreak.
Though I learned
it didn't taste much like anything,
when the bottle runs dry.

I put my hands on the counter
bracing myself
trying to focus on Death's face
but I couldn't focus on anything,
let alone stand on my own,
and I put my head in my hands
tears filling up the empty glass beneath me.

She sighed and looked at me with pity
and looked up at her in anger,
I didn't want her pity
or anyone else's.
I only wanted her to do her job,
but she refused me,
again.

Nights passed
and bottles came and went,
but yet, she denied me an early grave,
trying to tell me it wasn't time,
but it felt like time.

I felt like my bones were breaking
like all my blood was on fire
and I wanted Death to extinguish the flames.
So, I fueled the fires with alcohol,
it didn't take away the pain I had
but for a brief moment,
sometimes it felt like it did.

So I opened another bottle.

A Late Night Visitor

I thought I was safe
tucked away in my bed,
but late one night
I heard a knock at my bedroom door.
The dog didn't stir
and my husband lay fast asleep,
as if
only I could hear the eerie cries
coming from the other side.

I panicked
I tried to squeeze my eyes shut
but the cries didn't fade away,
they grew louder.

I slipped from the comfort of my sheets,
tiptoeing, shaking
nearing the door
the twist in my stomach became unbearable
and my hair stood on end,
as if I was being watched.

The world was asleep
as the clock crept on to strike 1:00a.m.
I froze in front of my door,
the cries had stopped
and I pressed my ear against the wood,
a voice rang from the other side,
telling me to come closer,
to let them in.

Against my own will
I placed a shaking hand around the door knob
and slowly turned it until a click
deafened my ears.
I pulled the door open,
just enough,
to peer around the corner.

I stole the oxygen from the room
and slammed the door shut,
I held it closed with my body,
as if I could keep it out.

"Let me in"
an old voice rasped,
the sound was haunting,
I hadn't heard it in years.
Yet here he was,
the devil at my bedroom door.

I was found.

My eyes flew open
and I could hardly catch my breath
a cold sweat breaking over my skin,
I was still in bed.

My husband fast asleep beside me
as if I had never gotten up at all,
but yet,
I heard that voice as clear as a bell.
I saw him,
as if he was standing right in front of me,
an unwelcome visitor.

Death's Last Visit

She smiled at Death
like an old friend
that came to say hello for the last time.
She opened her arms to embrace her
for time had kept them apart,
for far too long.

Many times Death came
to visit through the years
but she never stayed forever,
nor did she allow her new friend
to come with her.
It was never time.

From a young girl
to an elderly woman,
Death held her close in solis.
From a teenager damaged and bleeding,
to a woman wise beyond her years
heartbroken and now alone.

Death remembered the day her friend's world,
stood still.

Death stood in the back
draped in black behind the congregation.
She watched her friend mourn
as she wept for the love of her husband,
a soul now lost to the light.

The old woman never did recover.
The loss of her husband
was the loss of herself,
and her heartstrings broke
until there was only one left,
holding what little she had left inside her.

Seeing Death at the foot of her bed
was like seeing the sun for the first time
because she knew,
finally, she was going home,
and as that last string broke
the woman's heart stopped.

Death smiled.
For it wasn't a sad moment,
it was serendipitous,
she got what she always wanted,
to be free from this world
and to see her beloved once again.

More than anything,
she wanted to feel the love of her husband
and Death took the woman by the hand,
and led her into the light.

Her soul could finally rest
in the arms of the man she loved,
and they danced and danced
away into the clouds,
until they disappeared.

Death waved goodbye to her friend,
it was a lonely feeling
to watch her dance away,
but in one last visit
her job was finally done,
for her friend had finally come home.

Grief

She's the friend I could never let go of. It was comforting knowing I wasn't alone, even if it meant I was hurting inside.

I didn't know true Hell

until I was screaming

and no one was around to hear me,

until I was so cold

I could see my own breath

but no one else's,

until the music stopped

and there were no more chairs to sit in.

Then I knew,

that Hell was just being alone.

What Is It Like

What is it like
to ruin everything you touch,
to watch it crumble
rot,
and twist into something cruel.

What is it like
to lose everything you hold dear,
to watch your friends turn their backs
walk away,
and never return.

What is it like
to scream until your lungs are sore,
to bleed out
choke,
and still live to feel the pain.

What is it like
to feel everything all at once,
to feel a tsunami coming
and know,
that you're going to drown.

Brewing Storm

I wanted you so bad
it set my blood ablaze
but somehow,
even with fire flowing through my veins,
you managed to blow out my flame.
You were everything to me,
yet the feeling never quite felt the same.

You were hot
then you were cold,
over and over again
like a constant cycle that wouldn't end
and I was stuck in the middle.

It was exhausting,
I felt the butterflies in my stomach come alive
but then die so quickly
it made me sick down to my core.

All I ever wanted was to matter to you,
to be loved
craved,
to be chosen above all else.

I always believed that you loved me
but I admit,
it was a notion that was hard to hold onto,
even for me.

There were days
when I felt we could have danced
and been madly in love,
sadly,
we were nothing
but two storms colliding into one another,
neither willing to bend or break
and that was not love.

Our time was nothing but rainy days
filled with thunder
and lightening that seared the ground,
the love we had was just a dormant volcano
waiting to erupt
and burn us to ash.

Like Vesuvius molded Pompeii
into a cradle of endless devastation,
we too turned something beautiful
into something we, unfortunately,
could never forget.

The Break In

Hands shaking
fingertips bleeding, dripping
leaving behind bloody fingerprints
on crime scenes I didn't commit.

I catch my reflection in a mirror
and pause,
I am:
bloody
bruised
and tear stained.

I smear my hand across the mirror
wiping away the image
and refuse to believe that it's me,
but it is me.

My innocence broken into,
robbed.
It was so much worse,
so much more sinister
than I could let myself look at.

It was a violent sight to behold,
to be torn
vandalized
with a piece of me,
missing.

Black Ink

Grief never let me let you go,
I still remember sitting in dimly lit bars
laughing till the morning came
and it was time to go home.

I remember the beer you drank
and the cigarettes you smoked.

I remember the booth we sat in
and the smell of your leather jacket.

I remember the night
when we were sitting next to each other,
you looked over your shoulder
and there was a sharp glint in your eye.

You were wound up tight
so tense you were shaking,
gripping your beer, white knuckled
you moved your chair closer to me,
to block his view of me.

I raised a brow at you
and laughed,
you looked over at me
eyes as black as your hair,
you weren't laughing.

You were pissed that anyone had the audacity
to make me feel uneasy in your presence,
and I admired you for it,
it only made me love you more.

There was something inside you,
something I couldn't quite place
and I felt,
if I were to touch it,
it would burn.

We spoke of our dark desires
and the things we held dear,
we weren't so different
and the aches we had inside
drew us closer together.

Maybe, that's why the pain
and the loss
is something hard to let go of,
maybe that's why Grief won't let me forget.

Forget that I can get close to someone
and have memories,
but these memories hurt,
because he's not around anymore.

He was a lesson I had to learn
and I learned it the hard way.
Love did not live between us
like we thought it did,
and Grief will never let me forget it.

A Visit From Grief

"How do I handle life without him?
He was everything to me."
I asked Grief with tears in my eyes
and Grief answered,
"There is no way to handle it without him.
Though he is gone" Grief continued
"your heart will always leave a space for him
and because of this,
that hole will never really close
and will always ache for him."

I put my head in my hands and wept
because I did ache,
I hurt all over
and it felt so much bigger than a hole,
it was a gaping wound
that has been set on fire
and left to burn.

But Grief laughed,
"My dear child, let it hurt
let the pain sear into your soul
because one day,
I will not live here anymore."
As she pointed to my heart,
"I'll merely be a visitor
that brings you memories."

Grief reached into her robe
and handed me a drawing of his,
one that I burned long ago in rage.
I looked up at Grief and asked "Why?"
She simply said,
"because it once was special to you.
In a fit of anger you ripped it to pieces
and threw it into the flames.
Do you remember?"

I nodded, hanging my head in shame
weeping as I held the picture in my hands,
it was just a bird,
I remember the day he made it.
It was just for me,
and I destroyed its memory.

Grief sat with me
on a garden bench in Autumn
and held me close,
while I held that drawing to my chest,
and I cried
for the memories I had forgotten
and the good times I'll never get back.

I sobbed and asked Grief for the pain to stop
but she stroked my wind blown hair
and said, "When the pain is gone, so is the love.
If you want the pain to go away,
the love must leave with it."

My eyes widened with fear
as my heart tightened in my chest,
I had doubts festering within me
as I told Grief,
"I don't know how to stop loving him."

It was then I realized,
that this pain hurting me now
will one day fade away,
but losing my memories will always hurt,
and I didn't want to mourn forever.

Grief smiled and started to walk away
and I called after her,
I desperately didn't want to be alone.
She merely turned to me to say,
"You have loved and you have lost
but when you love again,
and you will,
this burden you carry will lessen.
Let it lessen, my dear
and give your heart a break."

She turned and continued to walk away
for her job was done for now
and Grief waved,
not a goodbye
but a see you later,
before she disappeared before my eyes.

That hole in my chest?
It didn't stop bleeding
but the pain did subside,
just enough,
just like she said
and somehow,
that made me miss her more.

Warrior

We have such a short time here,
to live
to love
and to lose.

The bravest of us live
even when we are ready to die.

So be brave
be courageous
be you,
because you are enough
to weather these storms
to fight in these battles
and come out victorious.

I know,
you're not quite ready for Death,
not yet.

But one day,
when you are old
and you are grey,
when you are ready to lie down at her feet
a valiant warrior,
you will receive her grace
and the quiet you fought so hard for.

Ghost

You haunt me
in the darkest depths of my soul,
you haunt me.
I hear whispers of my name
in the wind that sounds like your voice
biting at my ears
with words of times that have passed
and promises that turned out to be lies.

You haunt me
you're the shadow in every corner
everytime I turn around
there you are,
still standing behind me
breathing down my neck,
but when I turn
you're nothing but a ghost of my memories.

You haunt me
when I sleep, I dream
and there you are again.

I haven't thought of you lately,
I placed you in the back of my mind
and chained you there,
but somehow
you're here
and I awaken,
haunted still in another realm.

You haunt me
and I wonder,
if the pain will ever truly heal,
if I'll ever break the cycle
and be free from you,
because my heart is haunted by a ghost,
a spirit of someone who is gone
and hopefully,
never coming back.

You chased me.
Loved me.
Abandoned me.
Yet now,
you haunt me.

I wish your phantom would find a light
and be far away from me,
because still seeing your face in every crowd,
is driving me into madness
and I long for peace.

After years passed,
you haunt me still
and I hope,
once your ghost has departed,
that I will never miss you again.
It may feel like the first time you said goodbye
but this time,
I pray it'll be forever
so I may close the curtain
for this haunting's final finalé.

Last One

This is the last one,
the last time I'll write
and think of you with a pain in my chest,
because grief has held me captive long enough
and I'm tired of hearing your name
and seeing your face when I dream.

I don't want to think of you anymore
or the laughter you gave me
or the smile that spread across my face
when you held me tightly in your arms.

I want it all gone,
every last drop of happiness you gave
because what was it really,
a lie,
a game of cat and mouse.

All the while I was the mouse
and you were the cat,
catching and releasing me
again and again,
but I was a sick mouse
and I wanted to be caught
and I dreaded the release.

Each time I thought it would be different,
but you killed that part of me.
The hopeful part,
that thought,
our differences wouldn't tear us apart.

The Wall

"I just want to be left alone."

It's always such a pathetic lie,
because I never actually want to be alone
I want him to hear me screaming inside,
screaming not to leave me with my grief.

I need him in the worst way
but I remain behind a barricade,
looking out beyond a wall I cannot break down.
Not even for him
because if I break that wall down,
he will hear my screams
and he might run away.

Maybe,
he should run away
run as far away from me as he can
because there's tar leaking from me
and I don't want to trap him in the dark with me.

Sometimes, I feel as though
I should be the one running away
because the pain that has broken me,
broke me beyond repair
and I feel like I'm not a safe place to rest.

Virus

When it all becomes too much
and my sickness
begins to trickle down my cheeks,
I hope he remembers the real me.

I hope he doesn't forget the flowers
or my favorite flavor of ice cream.

I hope he can hear my cries for help
even when there's nothing but silence.

I hope he's never angry
on the days I can't get out of bed.
When the house is a mess
and I don't have the strength to open my eyes.

I hope he understands
that while Grief is a friend,
she is also selfish
and she holds me close against her,
never wanting to let go.

Like a mother to a sick child,
she clutches me tightly
and I suffocate from the weight of her love.
I think I'm safe here with Grief
but in reality,
I'm trapped in my own tomb.

<u>Time</u>

Years passed and I hurt all over. I thought the pain would be endless, then you came, and the sun began to shine on this dying garden. I fell madly in love, the agony blurred, and you were all I could taste.

I wish I were somewhere cold

and raining.

Somewhere that felt like an endless Autumn,

where time stopped in his tracks.

A place where Summer didn't live,

Spring never lasts

and Winter visited often.

One Winter's Night

Time was lost.
He traveled the world looking
searching
and longing
for a place to rest,
a place to call home.

He came knocking on my door one day
and I let him in,
it was the dead of Winter
the stars shined
and he shivered from the cold.

I took his coat
and Time stared at me
and took me in as I was,
a mess.
Cheeks flushed
and eyes red,
it was obvious
I had been crying prior to our meeting
and I looked away.

But Time took my face in his hands
and stroked the tears from my cheeks,
it was the softest I'd ever been touched
and suddenly,
I ached for a handsome visitor,
who only knew the color of my eyes.

Time may have felt lost
but in that moment,
I felt lost in Time.

He made a home in me,
Time knew of my memories
and saw the scars etched into my skin,
but chose to stay.
He enjoyed being needed,
being chosen,
and I needed him
more than I could have ever imagined.

We stayed up late
made love often
and spoke of dreams yet to come true.
Time longed for a home
much like I did,
and we built one together,
so neither would be alone again.

I fell in love with Time,
he healed the parts of me that hurt
and with him,
the bleeding stopped.
Time fit perfectly into my heart
and I into his,
like we were two souls separated long ago.

Together, with Time
bullet holes began to close
scars faded
and the nightmares that stole my dreams,
started to slip away.

Time was what I was longing for,
watering the love that bloomed flowers
that came from my broken heart,
he danced me away into the night
and I forgot,
that I was ever hurt before.

Time was no longer lost,
he fell in love with a grieving girl
who let him in some Winter's night ago,
and day by day
he loved her with all that he was,
with all that he had
because all that he had, was all that he was.

He was Time.

Missing Piece

In that moment,
standing in the kitchen
soft music playing in the background,
you were all I could see
blurred through salted tears
that fell and trickled down my cheeks.

I was drowning in the blue of your eyes
and swimming in the bravado of your voice
while you professed your love for me.
I soaked you in like you were living sunshine,
and I was a dying flower waiting for rain.

Your voice cracked
when you told me you love me
and your eyes told the truth painted in red.
You couldn't hold in your tears,
the love you had for me overflowed
and broke the dam you tried to hide behind.

You pleaded with me to stay with you forever,
like a dying man pleads with God for salvation.
I never wanted to be anywhere else more,
I wrapped my arms around you
and buried myself in you,
I could hardly breath
but I squeezed you as tight as I could
hoping it was some kind of silent promise,
one you could take to the grave.

You told me those magical words
"You're the one"
and I melted deeper into you,
but there was no greater pleasure
that compared to hearing
that I was the missing piece of you,
the part of yourself that you've searched for
and needed all this time.

Like we were two long lost lovers,
finally finding each other
after centuries of looking across the stars,
we found one another.

In that moment,
all I could do was kiss you
and hope that you could taste my love,
and know,
that there will never be anyone else but you.

Flesh of Eden

One kiss,
that's all it took
and you brought me closer to Heaven,
but when you looked up at me
eyes longing
and brimming with lust,
you made me want to do ungodly things to you.

The only Hell there is for me
is the torture I feel when I can't touch you.
The agony brings me to my knees
when your lying next to me
naked to the cold air in the room,
skin begging to be warmed by my hands
and my hands only.

When you shiver with need
and moan my name,
that is my deliverance.
For God gave me you
as an Eden on Earth,
my own holy sanctuary
wrapped in soft, intoxicating flesh.

The Love of Time

Time was bleeding in my arms
and my tears couldn't mend his wounds,
I wailed in pain for him
and the things I knew,
I'd never get back if I lost him.

He healed me when I was broken,
held space for me when I needed to breathe,
and always was a place I could rest
when the world was dark
and I needed his light to illuminate the way.

Time gave me everything
and asked for so little in return.
He was a simple man
only asking for the love he gave,
to be returned back to him.

I gave him everything I was
hoping, praying
it was enough,
because I needed his love.
His affection made me feel as though
I'd never be alone again,
and the fear of being without him,
brought me to my knees.

The Softest Parts of Her

I find her soft in the finest details
from the pout of her mouth
to the curves of her body
and even the way her hair falls around her face.
I have seen her wear her softness like a blanket
wrapped in nothing
but the air around her,
she's absolutely beautiful
and she doesn't even know it.

But I do.

She's breathtaking when she's soft,
from her heart that's only mine
to the heat between her thighs
and the way her lips feel
grazing along my jaw,
there is no part of her that doesn't call to me.

I can lay her in our bed
and know that I am right where I belong.
Her voice is all that I need,
to hear her plead my name
and in that single moment,
she is all that I can see.

I could devour her
but I prefer to take my time,
and savour the sweetest taste of love
that pours from her heart for me.
She deserves to feel my weakness for her,
to be loved tenderly,
in a way that only I can.

I ache for the way she says "I love you"
through gasping breaths
and desperate kisses,
feeling her skin wrapped around mine.

It's made unbearable when she's shaking,
digging her fingers into my arms,
and she whimpers my name.
Then the world stops
and I'm lost in everything that she is.

I can't see her eyes in the dark
but I know they're looking up at mine,
as she's trying to catch her breath,
she smiles at me
and I know,
I'll never be anything but hers.

Goodbye

It was a midnight sky
the day I told them goodbye,
Death sat to my left
and Grief to my right.

We talked until the stars came out
and laughed until the sun began to rise
of the life I used to live
the boys I used to love
and the ways I wanted to die.

What fond memories that they have become
to know,
that through all these years
I can cry from laughter
instead of pain
from the stupid mistakes I made
to thinking,
there couldn't possibly be anything better.

What I needed most was Time,
he came along to join us
and the world just made sense.

Death didn't stay long after
she was only there to check on my health,
and Grief, my oldest friend
did not come to stay,
she came to bring the old memories
but when she left
she took them with her this time.

Only Time remained when dawn broke
and I laid my head on his shoulder,
with a snap of his fingers
he made the misery disappear
and with a raise of his hand,
he brought my demons to their knees.

He gave me peace
and most importantly,
he gave me hope
when there was none left.

So, I finally said goodbye to my friends.
It was many years
until I caught a glimpse of Death again,
we merely smiled and waved,
like old friends would.

While Grief visited more often than Death,
we were always closer,
I was never sad to see her go.
At the end of our moments together
I would go running back to Time
and he would make the tears vanish
and remind me,
why I ever left the past where it belonged,
behind me.

<u>Acknowledgments</u>

Where to even begin...this has been a whirlwind of a year for sure! From just publishing my first piece of work "Sitting Under a Black Sun: A Collection of Poems" back in March, to now publishing my second book, just a few months later!

Poetry is an emotional roller coaster, as it should be. It's not for everyone and that's okay, but if you've made it this far, thank you! Seriously, thank you for reading the words that most people couldn't imagine having to write. Poetry can be gut wrenching and that's not a bad thing, to feel something is to be human. I always said that even if I only resonate with one person, that if I can make one person feel like they weren't alone, then I did what I set out to do with my writing.

My biggest thanks to my husband for just accepting that I'm constantly writing something here or there, even when I should be paying attention (oops). For being at every event and signing that he can. For being there for each chapter that was hard to write, and for letting me bounce ideas off of him all the time-even though he has no idea what's going on in my head. Which, let's be honest, is probably a good thing. He's been there from my first rejection, to my first publication, and now as I'm finishing book #2!

To my author bestie, DR Barnes, I love you so much! You're a constant inspiration to keep doing the damn thing. You've been more than supportive of my writer's journey and I could never thank you enough for that. Thank you for being there for me, answering all my questions, and just being one of the best friends I could have asked for, for all these years.

Thank you to all my friends and family for their support and for getting their hands on my first book! You guys have been amazing! Plus, a very special thank you to our local heroes at the Carlyss and Moss Bluff fire departments for their support through this adventure I've set out on!(My husband's co-workers are THE BEST) It has been a challenge for sure but you guys have made it all worthwhile.

My love for poetry will never die but let's just say, there will be more things coming from me in the years to come! We're gonna be switching gears for a bit while I'm working on my current WIP. Don't worry, I'll still be around to answer my emails, go to book signings and events, and still post silly little poems and blurbs on my socials.

Until the next one!
Happy Reading

Follow Along

You can follow me on socials like Instagram, Facebook, and Threads!

Instagram: @s.e.sumpter_poet

Facebook Page: Author S.E. Sumpter

Threads: s.e.sumpter_poet

You can also reach out to me through my author's email!
(Website is still under construction, but feel free to give it a look and let me know how I can improve it or what you'd like to see on it!)

Email: themoodybooksociety@gmail.com

Website: www.themoodybooksociety.com

Friend Support

Don't forget my bestie!
She has something great about to
come out so stay tuned for
something new!

While you're waiting in
anticipation,
pick up her current novellas,
"Wild Thing" and "Bareback"
and give her a follow on her
Facebook Page: Author DR Barnes